Cinderella

Manufactured in the U.S.A.

8 7 6 5 4 3 2 1

ISBN 1-56173-913-8

Cover illustration by Sam Thiewes

Book illustrations by Susan Spellman

Story adapted by Jane Jerrard

Publications International, Ltd.

O nce upon a time, there was a young girl, as sweet as sugared milk, as kind as a mother's kiss, and as pretty as a sun setting in the sky.

The young girl had a mean stepmother who made her life a misery. The stepmother and her two nasty daughters treated the girl as a servant. They made her scrub the floors and wash the dishes and pick up after them. They called the girl Cinderella because at day's end she would sit among the cinders on the hearth and warm her tired bones.

Cinderella was always cheerful and polite, though her stepsisters treated her cruelly. Her kindness made her beautiful, and her beauty shone like sunlight through her dirty face and ragged clothing.

One day, something very exciting arrived. It was an invitation to the Prince's fancy ball! All the fine people in the land were invited, and the sisters worried about what to wear and how to behave with royalty.

Poor Cinderella sewed and ironed for days, but she herself was not going to the ball. After all, she was reminded, she was only a servant. Besides, she did not have a ball gown to wear.

Finally, the great night arrived. As Cinderella helped her youngest stepsister into her gown, the cruel girl asked, "Cinderella, why don't you come with us to dance with the Prince?"

The stepmother and her daughters laughed at the thought of dirty, barefoot Cinderella dancing with the handsome Prince.

As the stepmother and her daughters rode off to the ball, Cinderella cried a few tears. Suddenly, a beautiful fairy magically appeared. It was Cinderella's Fairy Godmother!

"What is wrong, dear Cinderella?" asked the Fairy Godmother. For though she had secretly watched over Cinderella's hard life, this was the first time she had ever seen the girl cry.

Cinderella explained that she wanted very much to go to the ball and meet the Prince.

"And so you *shall* go, Cinderella, for you have always, always been good!" said the Fairy Godmother.

With her special magic, Cinderella's Fairy Godmother turned a hollow pumpkin into a beautiful coach. Then she found six mice, and waving her magic wand over them, she turned them into six fine gray horses, ready to pull the coach. All that was missing was a driver—and a fat white rat was just the thing!

"Now, sweet girl, you can go to the ball!" said the Fairy Godmother.

"But my clothes...," whispered Cinderella. "I cannot go to the ball in dirty rags!"

With one touch of her sparkling wand, the Fairy Godmother turned Cinderella's old dress into a lovely gown trimmed in gold and silver. Best of all, she gave the girl a pair of tiny glass slippers that fit just right!

With the help of the driver, Cinderella stepped into the waiting magical pumpkin coach. A shiver of excitement ran through her. Was this only a dream? She pinched herself and decided that it was not.

Just before the coach pulled away, Cinderella's Fairy Godmother spoke. "You must be home by midnight, Cinderella," she warned, "because my magic will disappear when the clock strikes twelve o'clock midnight!"

Cinderella promised that she would not be late, and off she rode to the ball. Her heart was pounding!

inderella stepped out of her coach and gracefully climbed the stairs to the Prince's palace. When she appeared in the doorway to the ballroom, the other guests hushed as she was escorted down the staircase.

The Prince took one look at her and was quite taken with beautiful Cinderella. In fact, everyone at the ball loved her. As the Prince and Cinderella danced, all the people smiled and watched. Even her stepsisters and stepmother did not recognize her!

The Prince asked Cinderella to dance every dance that night. Cinderella was so happy she forgot the time. The clock had nearly finished striking the hour of midnight when Cinderella remembered her promise to her Fairy Godmother.

$\mathcal{C}$inderella dashed out of the ballroom, leaving the Prince and the rest of the guests astonished! She ran down the palace steps in such a hurry that she lost one of her glass slippers.

The Prince ran after Cinderella, but it was too late. She had disappeared into the shadows. He wanted to call out to her, but realized that she had never told him her name! The Prince found the glass slipper on the palace steps, though, and he vowed to find its mysterious owner.

Cinderella ran all the way home dressed in her rags that night. Her magical coach had turned back into a pumpkin, and the mice and the rat had all run away. All that was left of her beautiful outfit was the other glass slipper.

The next day, everyone throughout the land could talk of nothing but the wonderful ball and the beautiful stranger who had stolen the Prince's heart.

But the Prince was very unhappy. He had fallen in love with a wonderful girl, but did not know her name or anything about her.

"This tiny glass slipper is all I have," he thought. "I must use it to try and find her." And that very day he began to search over all the land, trying to find the girl who could wear the tiny, delicate glass slipper.

The Prince and his servants went from house to house, inviting every woman—young or old—to try on the slipper. But not one foot could fit into it!

At last, the Prince arrived at the house where Cinderella lived with her stepmother and stepsisters. He was weary from his search and beginning to think he would never find the girl he loved.

The stepsisters both tried to fit their large feet into the slipper. It was plain to see that these ladies were not the mysterious girl from the ball.

Cinderella had been watching from her place by the fire. She asked softly, "May I please try?" Her stepmother and stepsisters laughed and told her not to waste the Prince's precious time.

The Prince knelt and held the glass slipper for Cinderella. Her foot slipped into it with ease! Cinderella had carefully kept the other glass slipper. Now she pulled it from her apron pocket and put it on, too.

The stepmother and stepsisters could not believe their eyes.

"It fits!" shrieked the stepmother and stepsisters.

"It fits!" smiled the Prince.

"It fits!" sang the Fairy Godmother, who had been watching all along. She once again waved her wand and magically dressed Cinderella in a beautiful gown. Cinderella went back to the palace with the Prince, who was so overcome with love and joy that he married her that very day!